# Pirates

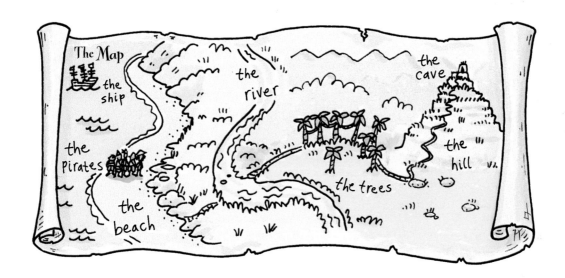

Written by Paul Shipton
Illustrated by Kelly Waldek

◌ Collins

Five big pirates went to the beach.

1 2 3 4

Four big pirates went to the river.

1 2 3

Three big pirates went to the trees.

Two big pirates went up the hill.

One big pirate went to the cave.

Five big pirates went back to the ship!

13

# The Map

the ship

the Pirates

the beach

the river

the cave

the hill

the trees

# 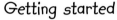 Ideas for guided reading

**Learning objectives:** Tracking the text in the right order; using a variety of cues when reading; knowledge of the story and its context; expecting written text to make sense and to check for sense if it does not

**Curriculum links:** Creative Development: Use imagination in role play and stories;

**Mathematical Development:** use number names in order

**High frequency words:** big, went, to, the

**Interest words:** pirates, beach, river, trees, hill, cave, ship, number words one to five

**Word count:** 43

## Getting started

- Ask children to say what they know about pirates. Make sure they know that pirates are sailors who are well known for greed and for hunting treasure.
- Read the title to the children and highlight the names of the author and illustrator.
- Turn to the title page. Ask children to talk about the map and prompt them to say what maps are for, particularly if you are a pirate!
- Walk through the text, looking at the pictures, up to p13. What are the pirates trying to do and what is happening on each page?

## Reading and responding

- Ask the children to read the book independently and aloud from the beginning up to p13. Prompt and praise correct matching of spoken and written words. Children could re-read for better understanding.
- Encourage children to make predictions and comments about the pirates. How many will there be on the next page? Why did he do that? Check that children can give reasons for their answers.
- When the children have read the story, turn to pp14–15. Ask the children to recap the pirates' journey, talking about what happened at each place on the map.